Lockdown Valentine

Michèle Laframboise

Lockdown Valentine

A Wow romance

 ECHOFICTIONS

Cover design by Echofictions
Original picture © Shutterstock /Chonnanit
Author portrait © Gilles Gagnon
End illustration by the author

This book published by : Echofictions
Mississauga, Ontario

www.echofictions.com

ISBN 978-1-988339- 78-8 (print)

Table of contents

for Kris Kathryn Rusch,
with my thanks

Lockdown Valentine

S NOWFLAKES HAD NO RIGHT fluttering in the sun like fairy dust, falling oh, so gently you would think Hardwood Street and its high-end fashion shops had been teleported inside a snow globe. The flurries floated down in lazy figure eights, each small and flawless, and shiny. A spectacle that would have been perfect one year ago.

Cerise Joseph pushed down the rim of her pink and violet fabric mask, sewn by her mother's skillful hands months ago. By offering her face to the dainty snowflakes, the young woman tried to dial back happier times.

When she was hoping instead of moping.

Nowadays, a vise of guilt was twisting her innards when she thought about her mother's empty apartment. She had visited to water the violets and the cat grass pot, and to leave a portion of kibble for the calico cat lounging on the second-floor windowsill.

Cerise pulled back her mask. No one had seen her and her portion of the sidewalk was empty, but she did not want to lower her guard with an everchanging virus.

She had dispensed with the glossy lipstick that complimented her brown skin. What use was it, hidden under a square of tissue? Not even mentioning blood-red smudges inside the gauze material…

Cerise pushed back the hair-killing knit hat to get a better sight of the sky, crisscrossed by electric lines and streetlights. From where came those slow-dancing flurries, she had no idea. Around her, the sounds of traffic and the smell of gas seemed subdued, muffled by the snow.

Of course, the Covid-19 lockdown had lowered the car density in downtown, but there were always exceptions. Or people who, thinking themselves exceptional, challenged the lockdown.

She almost bit her lips as anger welled inside her. To distract herself from those dark ideas, she tilted her head back to find out the generous cloud.

The sky was clear, luminous, devoid of any stormy mushrooming masses, except the faint outline of hair-like cirrus clouds at plane-altitudes. This fairytale, luminous snow seemed to materialize from nothing. The flurries were already covering the sidewalk with a fuzzy layer, so innocent in those first minutes, like her mom's light cough on the phone, a week ago.

A cold, just a cold, Vivi had said, with a warm lilt in her Haitian accent.

Cerise had hoped it was the simple flu, the kind that morphed your nose into a spigot. But the next day, when her mother's breathing became hurried and gurgling, and her headaches worsened, the two of them could not deny this was the bug.

It was fortunate, Cerise reflected bitterly, that her mom had not been afflicted with the stupid pride that infected certain dudes, that made them deny something was bad until it was too late.

She walked on Hardwood Street, *en route* to see her mother, on automatic pilot. At a point, she caught her reflection on a shop window: her orange polyester coat where the flurries melt, leaving moist prints; her matching orange knit cap, her dark wooly trousers; her practical walking boots. All shops were shut, and the rents would hit them hard.

As her mother had been hit, coughing her lungs off at the hospital.

Not because she was an inveterate smoker, but because an irresponsible clod without a mask had brushed by her in the store where she worked. Vivi has stepped away to increase the distance and pointed helpfully to the alley.

Of course he was carrying *the* bug.

As simple as that.

And as no good deed went unpunished, the nasty-sounding cough had come three days after the chance encounter. Of course, that chain of transmission had to be reconstructed from memory, at the hospital.

And there was no way to retrace the carrier...

A high-pitched squeal of brakes sliced her thoughts, so close the sound was almost physical.

Before the squeal ended, Cerise was swept back like a snow flurry. She was conscious of her boots brushing the hood of a black Mercedes, her knitted cap falling, her hair following, falling over her eyes.

Cerise had not flown away: someone had pulled her from the street corner.

She was conscious of the hands clamped over her upper arms, so tight her circulation had stopped. She twisted, meeting a pair of light blue eyes over a green mask sporting a yellow sun with rays. The Mercedes sped away, the driver annoyed by the near miss.

The hands released her.

That's when she connected the dots, and saw how she had been on the verge of crossing the street without looking. That stranger had bypassed the social distancing to pull her out of harm's way.

"Are you OK?" a man's voice asked, muffled by the fabric.

The stranger wore a white pullover with corded motives in the knitting, a pair of dark blue jeans (so dark she could almost smell the dye pigment) and one striped seaman cap, blue over white, that left his ears exposed. The clothes suggested a laid-back attitude, and they had been appropriate in the sun, before the fairy-tale snow started to fall.

A pair of marble-blue eyes pierced her almost to the bone, over a straight nose and chin hidden under the mask.

Something hit her right boot. A can of diced tomatoes had rolled from an upset canvas bag. And there, was that a box of Ritz crackers? The overturned groceries told of his haste to intervene.

Cerise sucked in air between her teeth, ashamed of herself.

The nervousness that had plagued her in high school rooted her, like a snow statue. She searched her words to make things right somehow, because it seemed suddenly important that something in this terrible day got better. But all that came from her mouth was the ubiquitous, lame reply.

"I'm sorry," she said, mumbling her words.

He bent his frame to retrieve his groceries, his bare hands picking up the apples and the crackers.

"And what made you so distracted you were about to cross a busy street on a red light?" he asked, from the other side of the large set of shoulders. "A boyfriend?"

His tone had morphed from annoyed to amused, but the question stung.

∽∾

OF COURSE, on this day of all days, any young woman would be on her way to a lover, not on her way to pass a long stifling hour looking at her swaddled mom on the bed, surrounded with machines, attended by nurses so wrapped in layers of uniform and clear plastic they looked like green candies.

The day before, Cerise couldn't even hold her mother's hand. All she could do was looking on from the other side of a dividing glass, with the doctor's words hanging like a curse in her mind: *We can only wait and see.*

She had given her cell's number to a nurse and dragged her feet, the kilometers of corridors and lifts and more corridor to the exit, the skin of her hands glistening with repeated splatters of alcohol disinfectant.

She could not bring herself to take the bus, nor a taxi, lest she contaminated the whole city with her sadness. Only her feet were thinking and they wanted to walk, just walk.

And that's when the weird, cloudless snow had started falling, in full sun.

And here she was, on the verge of tears, waiting for the overworked doc to call with the result of her own Covid-19 test, the one they had taken six days ago, when she brought her mother to the emergency.

No, the doctor with a tree's name (she couldn't remember it properly) wouldn't call. A text message would suffice to end, or prolong, her torture.

⁊∿⋞

IT SEEMED SO LUDICROUS HOW, on this day the previous year, a bright future loomed in front of Cerise like a promise: the training for the new sale job… and a fiancé from a wealthy family.

Her mother, a fan of theater, had justly pegged the man as a Lothario, the name derived from an old play featuring a foppish, unscrupulous seducer hiding under a charming façade.

A bubble of regret, of shame, rose from the young woman's stomach. She gulped to prevent the tears that threatened to well up. No job thanks to the lockdown, no well-heeled fiancé.

The utter injustice, and this blow to her hard-working mother, made her whole body tense. Cerise was conscious of her ragged, fast breathing, as anger threatened to submerge her self-control.

Her lips pressed, she violently shook her head. No. No lying boyfriend who promised a wedding in whites only to seduce her.

The mask's fabric stretched as the stranger worked his mouth under it.

"Look, I'm sorry," he said. "I didn't mean to pry."

His voice edged on a bass register that clashed with the lean frame (in her imagination all bass singers were barrel-shaped). It possessed a nasal component linked to winter, that only made him more flesh-and-bone, human, warm. And also more interesting.

Before she could let herself drift in a sea of possibilities, she saw a can shining under the edge of the sidewalk. The tomato paste can must have rolled farther from the bag, and dropped from sight.

She bent to retrieve it, her fingers closing on the small cylinder. Through her thin nylon gloves, she felt the metal, still warm from the grocery aisles. The Fresh-Deli tow doors back, or the vivid canary-yellow No Frills farther down the street? Probably the Deli, because of the reusable bag. Most big box stores had reverted to single-use plastic bags, under the guise of protecting the cashiers handling those.

As she turned to put the can back in the bag, she saw, peeking among the other boxes of tea, the familiar shape of a heart-shaped box of chocolates.

The box was obviously expensive, because the satin-like fabric covered it, a glorious scarlet that promise 80% cacao-rich goodness. Just to think of the succulent cherry-chocolates or the marzipan-filled balls made her salivate. The hospital eatery had been cordoned off to visitors, reserved for the (no doubt valiant) health care personnel. She had to make do with an egg-salad sandwich from the machines.

"Here," she said, to cover her trouble.

Of course, this handsome man would be on his way to a nice meeting.

She stretched her arm to avoid touching his wrist, glad for her gloves, so he would not have direct contact with her. Distributing Covid around was not in her plans.

As if he had guessed her intent, he propped up his bag (the twin curves of the chocolate box still jutting up) toward her to respect the distancing.

"Why, thank you!" he said, the wrinkles of his mask stretching sideways over a foot-wide smile.

The *Thank you* rose in a light-hearted inflection that immediately lifted her mood. The words seemed to brush tiny gravels in his throat. She raised her head, in time to catch the gleam in his eyes, maybe a trick of the sun.

She couldn't see his neck under the vivid red scarf wrapped around and tucked under the rim of the knitted pullover. Nor could see smell anything in the frigid air, except to ascertain he didn't wear any men's perfume they called Cologne. She started thinking about the lips under the mask.

Oh, how she would have loved to meet him last year!

Then, she cast off those thoughts. That fancy heart-shaped box was destined to someone else.

She steeled herself, a vessel powering on to leave his orbit, never to go back again. She molded her lips to say, *well, it's been nice meeting you,* and *thanks again for saving my life.*

Then, the first guitar accords of *Strawberry Fields Forever* rang from her handbag. The Strawberry tune served for her text messages notifications.

She felt the color leak from her face, not that she could see herself, but the loss sensation was so brutal she saw in her mind the red globules leaving her extremities to take refuge in her heart.

"Excuse me," she said, a polite reflex, as she turned from him to fish in her bag.

৵৵

THE RUBBER ENVELOPE of the phone felt warm under her fingers as she pulled it and press the side to light the screen. Yes, indeed, the hospital indicator and the doc's name, Aspen, were blinking.

"Something wrong?"

The warm bass voice came from miles away, drowned under the pulse beating on her temples, under the throbbing of her heart. She took a small breath and looked up the screen to know her fate.

She read the words, not believing.

Please call, the words said. *We need your consent.*

Not her result at all. *Consent.* Infinitely worse. And the number.

Cerise took a ragged breath, teetering over the event horizon of a black hole. Her mother. The too-cold, fast-moving air scraped her throat.

It could only be her mother. She pursed her lips to keep her hurt inside, but a whimper escaped.

That light snow coming from nowhere, her superstitious basement mind whispered, could it be…?

The white pullover stranger must have talked but she didn't hear any words. The street, the shops and his half-face all blurred under the tears welling up and the thought of a future without her mom exploded in ragged, wracking sobs.

৵৵

CERISE HAD NEVER BEEN IN FAVOR of displaying her emotions in public, a hallmark of her that was half poise, half timidity. But that message had blown up her dam, nothing to be done but run for cover and count the damage later.

Last year, at this point, there would have been arms around her, and soothing words murmured in her ears. The Lothario had been good at whispering platitudes. This was before the break-up, of course.

Their affair had lasted longer than he had intended to. They were or, rather, he was, preparing a month-long prenups journey visiting the European capitals. As he was at odds with his rich father, Cerise had pitched in to help him buy the plane tickets to Paris…

Until, one day before their departure date, his phone number went dead. No other way to reach him, and the AA counter clerk, when she called the company, told her both tickets had been rescinded into a first class seat, departing… the previous morning.

She searched on the web, but he had vanished, as if he had never existed. As she now suspected his rich family never did. Her mother had been the one seeing through him, of course. And now, Vita-Maria was lying, dying on a bed, contaminated by a careless buyer.

Cerise sniffed. She fished in her coat pockets for the Kleenex pack. Her fingers closed on empty air.

"Here," the white pullover man said. "Take this one. Never used."

She felt something pressed on her palm. It was not a Kleenex, but a plastic sandwich bag with a pad of gauze, the kind slipped as an inner layer inside a mask.

"But," she said.

"I've got a bunch of those, don't worry," he said, tapping a bulging pocket in his jeans. "I need to change them often," he added, his voice down a half-octave, the lightness leached out.

She pulled the bag open and used one pad to dab at her eyes. Clarity returned. The faint snow was falling, but the flurries were smaller, and in lesser numbers. She thought maybe the magic was going away, when she needed it so much.

The stranger was balancing on the balls of his feet, a pair of thick-soled sport shoes, his bag nestled like a child in the crook of his elbow. (The child simile came naturally, as she had lain in such position in her mothers arms.)

"Look, he said, I can tell you need to call someone. It's cold, and my things can wait a bit. Why don't you make this call inside?

His free hand pointed to the façade of a Lazy Lounge Café, a small, warm place Cerise had favored at the time of her studies.

She must have nodded without thinking about it, because the next thing she knew, they were inside the art deco style Café, sitting on plush chesterfields that would be a drag to disinfect after they left, with a low, glazed-top table brushing their knees.

She reveled in the plush seat, in the warm atmosphere filled with coffee and sugar biscuits scents. There were only two other clients at this non-rush hour, seated well apart. The glazed table between them ensured a safe distancing.

The warmth spreading in her limbs made her conscious that, if she hadn't put her life in danger, forcing his intervention, she could have kept on walking and walking in the freezing cold, and gained a serious chill back home.

She turned to wrap her coat on the high dossier. While doing so, she was conscious of his gaze resting in her. However, it was nothing like the loaded gazes locked on her in the streets and public places, BC.

The way those blue eyes looked at her felt rather like a soft coverlet draped over her shoulders, both amiable and protective. The man was simply sitting in his plain pull over, the grocery bag at his feet.

If she keened on her left, she could even see the red of the chocolate box.

"I'm Michael," he said.

And then he removed his mask.

∼∾

CERISE ALMOST FORGOT to respond with her name. He was that gorgeous.

Maybe even Hollywood-gorgeous. When he removed his cap, his thick brown hair exploded outward, the bangs stopping short of the blue eyes. The hair only emphasized the symmetry of his face, the straight nose, the strong chin.

He was as Caucasian as she wasn't, but in the 'central Russia mountains area' sense. His jutting cheekbones and fleshy lips suggested a Slavic ancestry. Why, he had the physic to play an agent of the KGB, or whatever the Russian agency was called now, on movies.

But his wide, generous smile made all the secret agent stud vanish.

"I'll order coffees, while you make your call," he said, rising, hiding the smile under his mask. "Sugar, cream, milk?"

"Milk," she said, still dazed.

When he walked to the counter, she wondered about his age. Like many Slavic ascent people, his unlined face placed him any decade between twenty and fifty. But here was a suppleness in the way he moved, an expressivity in his arm gestures when he talked to the barista, that brough him closer to her own age.

She looked down at the ceramic tiles tracing flowers on the table, and took her phone. Even if Michael was on his way to his lover (and it might be a man, she had no way to tell) at least, she wouldn't be alone when the hammer fell.

Cerise punched the numbers, painstakingly. Then she waited for the dispassionate robot machine to list the choices. She punched the extension number, and was relieved to hear a woman's cool soprano voice. Cerise began to ask for Doctor Aspen, but the cool voice spurred on, and she understood this was another conversational robot.

Then she had to wait again to be connected, while a background Muzak rendition of *Moon River* grated her right ear.

A coffee landed on her table. She nodded at him, appreciating how he had asked for china mugs instead for going for the wax paper cups.

Michael sat there, sipping his own coffee, his gaze roaming over the street outside the window. She wondered whose lucky person he was going to bring those chocolates for, and about... a lot of things she itched to know about him. His line of work. His family. Was he an immigrant like her mother and herself? Had his family established roots in this new ground?

She stowed those questions under a mental rug. She was not ready to let another man in her life.

Not now.

స~ఆ

THE WAIT LENGTHENED. It had already been bothersome BC, before Covid.

But she knew people were dying in the hospital, and the health workers were run ragged, with the variants of the bug playing havoc with the best laid plans. Poor doctor Aspen (and his nurses) was probably juggling a dozen intensive-care patients, or maybe he had finished his shift and his replacement was updates on the cases.

On Vita-Maria Joseph's case.

Her strong mother, who had survived the social unrest after the dictature, who had brought her daughter through college, asking nothing in return…

The colored tiles on the table blurred.

Cerise was crying, and this time she did not hide her tears.

"Hey."

That call, said so softly no one could hear it. One syllable, that said so much more, like: You're not alone. She turned the phone to keep it on her era, but the speaking mike away.

"It's my mom," she said in a whisper, as if the bug would get nastier if she raised her voice.

She wasn't the kind to blurt out. He just nodded, his eyes misted.

More waiting, more sips of cooling coffee.

Then the annoying Muzak stopped. Hope swelled in her heart as she heard a series of clicks.

And the line wend dead. She listened to the tone, disbelieving.

The shock must have registered on her face. Michael's expressions grew pensive.

"They are too busy," he said. "Pressed like lemons. I wish I could help, but medicine's not my field."

"And what is your field," she asked before she could think.

"Mechanical engineer. I'm one of the lucky employees who can work from home, so I call my own hours."

"Well, it must be practical for visiting your, er, friend," she said, pointing to the red chocolate box.

Cerise berated herself for her nosiness. She was not entitled to this guy. He had a significant other already. She took up the coffee mug, to find it empty.

"I, I think I'll have to go now," she said.

"It's a good distance from here."

He rose, in a sinuous move, his face lit up from inside.

"Tell you what, Cerise. (He tapped the bag.) If you accompany me for a small errand, just a short walk, I can drive you to the hospital after. I'm parked not far from here."

Cerise blinked, surprised by the volubility. So she would accompany him to his lover's flat and look at him delivering the heart-shaped box? She surprised herself by accepting.

This Valentine Day was getting weird and weirder.

THE SNOW HAD DWINDLED to a few isolated flurries when she followed him across the Hardwood avenue shops. He stopped once to buy a small rose bouquet (while she waited outside so only one of them got in the store).

He held the wrapped bouquet in a protecting arm as he guided her along another street, then to a quaint, red-bricked apartment building that stood beside a carwash. Three stories, probably twelve flats.

Not the fanciest place to live, Cerise thought, as she considered the rusted iron grid balconies gracing the facade. That place was a hold out of the fifties, pale yellow bricks and a jutting extension covering the small staircase of the entrance.

Through the glass of the inner door, she spotted black smudges on the hall's brown rug, and chocolate bar wrappings lay about.

Michael put down the canvas bag to push the round number nine button, using a handkerchief so he didn't left any virus on the surface. The sound system crackled with parasites so the voice on the other side was barely audible. Michael just said "Elly, I'm here" and the inner door buzzed one half-second later.

Elly. Cerise pictured a voluptuous, black-haired Elisabeth Taylor-type. A pang of envy swept through her. She hadn't dressed for job interview today, too unnerved by her mother's health situation.

They went through the door, keeping their distance and their masks on. They used the stairs instead of the lift, which led Cerise to lower her age estimate to the healthy thirties.

Michael did not even look winded as they stepped on the third floor landing, he still carrying the heavy canvas bag.

Cerise braced herself when they stepped in the short hall. She was about to meet Michael's lover, which was a major rung on the awkwardness scale. But then, it beat being dumped by the Lothario.

The door of apartment number Nine was ajar, a Hallmark's flowery 2021 calendar pinned on the inside.

She had to stay calm so this Elly would not see her as a threat.

Michael stepped through the threshold, so all she saw around his wide back was a portion of a well-maintained appartement with jaunty lime-green walls and a couch the same shade of green as the walls.

She followed him inside, her features molded into the benign, innocent expression she had used as a child after she had committed some mistake.

A cheerful voice rose inside the flat.

"Why, Michael! You shouldn't have brought those flowers!"

"It's to make amends, since I can't stay long, Ellie," Michael said.

"And chocolates, too? Really?"

"You know you're my sweet Valentine, El!" Michael said, his voice caressing.

When Michael carried the canvas bag to the small kitchen nook, Cerise got her first sight of the dreaded rival.

Ellie sat on the sofa in her dark blue pajama, one leg propped up on a stool. Her ankle was wrapped in clean bandaged, like a water polo ball. She wore a chirurgical mask, a N-95 and fine-rimmed glasses that enlarged her gray eyes. A can of clear disinfectant liquid and a flat box of wipes lay on the low coffee table, next to a pile of glossy magazines.

She was turning the red chocolate box, not heeding the noise as Michael tinkered in the small kitchen, cupboards doors opening and shutting, containers pushed around on the refrigerator shelves.

When she noticed her other visitor, Ellie's smile raised a fine network of lines under her white puffy hair.

"And you brought a friend! How nice!"

Michael set the flowers on the small dining table. He had grabbed a clear glass pot the right size, another sign that he knew his way around the kitchen.

"Yes, but it is because of her that I can't stay long," he said.

When Ellie raised her whispery eyebrows in question, he added, quickly, sending an apologetic glance to Cerise.

"She has a… family emergency," he said.

He blew a kiss, his puckering lips pulling the fabric of the mask.

"But I'll make up for it, next week, promise!"

ॐॐ

CERISE CAST A GLANCE UPWARD when they exited the building. The light snow had not returned, chased away by a light breeze.

She saw a pale blue paper mask rolling on the yellowed grass, probably from the bus stop. She hated this new littering habit, because unwary children could pick those up and get infected. Without breaking stride, she bent and grabbed one cordon of the blue mask. The mask was rather clean, devoid of any smudge, but it was a false perception, as the enemy decimating a part of humanity could be hiding in the oh-so-white paper.

When she looked up, she surprised a grateful look on Michael's cerulean eyes. And that gratitude spread like a physical web between them. She became aware that this simple act of kindness, of looking out for others, linked them.

"There's a bin just by my car, there," he said, pointing to a white Subaru, the flanks dusty with caked salt.

Michael's voice felt like a warm, protective blanket.

He had parked on Elli's street, and there was a handy wastebasket close by.

When she got in, she was surprised to find the interior pleasantly warm. The windshield had greeted the sun rays. The car smelled of hot plastic and lemon-scented disinfectant. In such closed quarters, she could guess he had used a whey-scented shampoo for his hair, and his body warmth had spread to the wool of the pull, producing a pleasant, homely scent.

A few minutes later, he was negotiating the mounting traffic downtown. She sat on the back seat, on the passenger side to maximize the distancing.

Cerise was had barely come down the rollercoaster of emotions when she had found out who the mysterious woman was.

While he was inspecting the refrigerator for any food passed their best-before date, Ellie had explained how she had slipped over a patch of ice while returning from her groceries. The hospital was packed chock-full with Covid-19 patients, so Ellie had been summarily treated for the worst, bandaged and discharged. With her leg, she couldn't leave her home. So she had called Michael.

"It was, um, kind of you to do that," she said, to break the silence.

"Many older folks are left alone, and vulnerable," he said. "So a couple of friends and me have formed a small team to bring groceries and a bit of comfort to isolated people."

"You're like a Boy Scout," she said.

Cerise regretted those flippant words, as soon as they escaped her. But her whole being was flipping on and off, like a dime spinning on a table. Sorrow, for her mom. Joy, for this man driving with a sure hand.

He let a short snort through his mask.

"You could say that. My dad was a Cubs leader in his time."

She cringed inside, afraid her uncaring words would snap this frail link between them.

"I didn't mean to laugh at you," she said. "My Mom put me in the Girls Guides for two years. I loved it. But…"

She fell silent.

Michael jerked the wheel, to avoid a car doing a lane change without checking his blind side. The swerve forced her to grab the headrest in front of her.

"But what?" he asked, truly interested.

She kept her grip on the cushioned headrest, to stabilize her.

"Well, it's like, too many grow out of it. Once adults, they lost the, well…, the spark."

"I see what you mean," he said, his eyes on the road. "There were good things in the movement, despite the scandals. The ideal of brotherhood, of the service."

They kept silent, because driving required more concentration closer to the heart of the city.

Cerise took advantage of the downtime to consult her phone. No new message had registered.

This could be equally good, because if Vivi's condition had taken a bad turn, they would have called her, or bad, because maybe they were waiting for her consent to remove the respirator, because so many needed it.

And she was still waiting for her test results.

She closed her eyes and let the gentle hum of the engine and the tug of gravity rock her left and right, as he changed lanes. In a few minutes, she would take her leave of this gallant man, and receive her answers. So she let herself sink against the safety belt, let her gaze roam the facades and trees and lampposts going by, like she did as a child, when her father was with them.

The Subaru turned into the parking lot next to the hospital, the visitor's spaces with the sky-high prices. She tapped the dossier of his seat.

"No, no! You can just leave me on the sidewalk here," she said. "No need to pay a fortune for a few minutes!"

But he was already lowering his window and taking the slip from the parking's electronic post. When he inched the Subaru in a free space, he killed the engine.

"Cerise, I had two family members ill from the Covid, last year. My dad almost died. It was a torture for my mom. So I know what you're going through."

He exited the car, and had rounded the nose to open her door.

"What I'm telling you is, you don't have to endure this alone," he said, stepping back to let her exit.

He closed the door and locked the car with the key, the front lights flashing twice in response. He slipped the keys in his jean's pocket, his gaze also locked on her.

"And, well, you're worth more than a few minutes."

Her knees wobbled under the relief. She had not realized how hard that year had been after the Lothario had left her. But here, Michael was there, a solid presence that she could feel with her eyes shut. She cursed the bug that forbid her to nestle in his arms. If she was an asymptomatic carrier, she would keep away until the vaccine was distributed in their age group.

"I'll stick with you, that is, if you want me to."

He paused. They were at the glass doors, where a blue-clad assistant with a temperature scanner waited.

"Well, do you?"

Cerise, who had been scanning the array of painful decisions looming in her near future, blinked. Having him at her side, for more than a few minutes?

"Yes, yes!" she said.

THEY DID NOT HAVE TO WAIT LONG after Cerise had been waived through (she had no fever) and presented her card to the front desk. They were sent through a wide public area that would be normally filled with vending stands, jewelry, cards, artisanal gifts, that was empty save for an array of ribbons staking territories, marking safe distances. The ceiling ventilators were humming full spin.

The in-house fast-food outlets were take-out only, and staked out.

A volunteer, masked and clear-helmeted, directed them to an improvised office. When she and Michael stepped in, all she could smell was the nose-tingling liquid on her hands.

The doctor who greeted them on the other side of a desk was an older woman with glasses and a gentle expression in her dark eyes. A pair of dangerous silver hoops hung from her earlobes as she tapped on the keyboard of a thin computer. The flaring plastic cone covered her mask so only the (well-protected) hoops and eyes were visible. A plate with red numbers blinked at her hip.

As Cerise had guessed, the Dr Aspen had left, and the replacement had her own bursting backlog. The name on the ID card was Dr. Nyerere.

She propped up the phone screen with the message.

"What's this consent I have to give?" she asked in a trembling voice, smelling the sharp tang of the disinfectant spread in her hands.

The doctor blinked, behind her double barrier of glasses and plastic.

"Oh, poor you!" she said. "You didn't have any consent to give. Doctor Aspen had mixed up the phone numbers. We have so many Covid patients here, and he finished a twenty-hours shift."

"My, my mother, Vita-Maria Joseph…"

She couldn't bring herself to say more.

Michael's fingers closed on her hand. It was unexpected, this contact, not fairytale-like with his skin rendered papery by too many disinfectant applications. Both had liberally applied the nose-tingling, alcoholic lotion on their hands. But through all the sensory weirdness, his skin communicated warmth, and support.

Doctor Nyerere's smile widened.

"Ms. Joseph," she said, "your mother has been taken off the intensive care and moved to the medium care unit. It has been touch and go for a while, but she's breathing by herself and responding well to the treatment."

Cerise took a long ragged breath, as if to collect all the oxygen in the room. She felt tears rolling down her eyes to the fabric of her mask. In the blur, she locked on the white smudge.

While her mother's condition improved, hers might not. She braced herself to ask the next question.

"And, my own tests…?"

The doctor looked at her screen. Michael's fingers wrapped hers in wordless reassurance. Cerise's heart stammered wildly. Had she met the man of her dreams, just to die on him?

Then the word fell.

"Negative."

So, Vivi had not given her the virus. She felt like a giant hand had stopped squeezing her ribcage. The air escaped her lips in a question.

"Can I,… can *we* visit my mom?"

The doctor's hand went to her face, as if to scratch an itch, then stopped a finger length from her own protective equipment. The gesture made Cerise aware of all the irritations that stemmed from these constraints. Heroism came in various forms.

"I suggest you return after dinner," the doctor said. "Too many people in the corridors right now. Eight-o-clock should be better."

She looked at them, over her glasses.

"Are you her husband?" the doctor asked.

Michael let out a short chuckle.

"Not yet. We just met today."

"Ah," Dr. Nyerere said. "It's just, the way you're looking at each other… I guess you might have many more days in front of you!"

~♥~

THEY LEFT THE TINY OFFICE, in proper, distancing decorum. Inside, Cerise felt like burning inside with joy. She itched to feel his arms around her, but she had to be stoic, for both their sakes.

"Let's get something to eat, and see your mother. If you still want to present me."

Cerise smiled under her mask. She was hungry, too.

"You'd better keep your distance."

"Yeah," Michael said. "I'll have to wash my hands. And wait two long weeks before holding you in my arms."

Just as they were about to leave the wide public area, an in-house pharmacy outlet, she spied a clear doorway on a frame.

It was a curtain of clear plastic with bulbous cartoony appendages hanging out. Drawing closer, she saw that it was a hugging curtain, as a mother was hugging one pajama-clothed child, with a masked nurse keeping watch.

Both were not wearing masks, since the curtain acted as a separation. She hadn't noticed the apparatus before (but then, she hadn't had any need of it.)

"Michael, let's not wait two week for our first embrace."

Later, after the nurse had disinfected the whole apparatus, Cerise and Michael faced each other, and removed their masks.

Again, she was stunned by his gorgeousness, and the generous lips she would get to know better soon. His smile told her he was not disappointed either.

They plunged their arms into the appendages, and groped for an optimal hug.

At first, the plastic partition felt awkward with the sharp sanitizer smell, but the four arms crossed, and she could feel his ribs and the hard curve of his shoulders, and a hollow in the neck where he could and the beating of his heart when they leaned one against the other.

It was, after all those months of solitude, the best hug ever.

When, at last, they reluctantly let go of each other (they were not the only ones needing a safe hug), Michael made a solemn promise that Cerise knew he would keep.

"In two weeks, you and I will catch up the lost time!"

THE END

Heartfelt Thanks

THIS BOOK IS THE BRAINCHILD of a writing exercise directed by Dean Wesley Smith. I aimed to give hope in the peculiar pandemic context.

అోఅ

LAST, BUT NOT LEAST, thanks to you, reader, for staying along for the ride. I hope you enjoyed the story. If you did, feel free to share your enthousiasm with your friends and leave reviews on your favorite platforms.

About the Author

WHEN NOT TRYING to initiate first contact with strange flora, Michèle Laframboise juggles her time between drawing comics and crafting stories.

A science-fiction lover since childhood, she has written 19 novels and more than 50 short stories, earning three Auroras and two Solaris awards.

Her works have appeared in *Solaris, Carmilla, Galaxies, Géante Rouge, Brin d'Éternité, Tesseracts, Fiction River* and *Compelling Science Fiction*. She has been translated into French, Italian and Russian.

Holding degrees in geography and engineering, she uses her scientific background to create worlds filled with humor, invention and wonder.

Official website:
www.michele-laframboise.com
in French and English

Humoristic blog:
sundayartist.wordpress.com

Publisher's website:
www.echofictions.com

 Echofictions

For some news and amusing reading reviews, join
 Michele's happy band of readers!

http://michele-laframboise.com/fans

Other books by Michèle

Change or die!

Science-fiction / humor / First contact

Loongunis need constant fluctuations to thrive, while the strange-haired Earthmen hate the endless unstability.

When a sabotage impairs the shift engines of their traveling Box, the enforced immobility might drive all Loongunis mad...unless their translator can work out a solution!

Science fiction adventure at its best, a quirky 7000-word story told by multiple award-winning author Michèle Laframboise.

How to Think inside the Box
978-1-988339-40-5 (print)

Trapped in the most beautiful place on earth...

Humor / mystery / Ornithology

Equipped with her Sibley Guide and trusty binoculars, Amanda Byrd pursues the most elusive winged species. As she explores a beautiful canyon at dawn, Amanda discovers their lift sabotaged, trapping their group at the canyon's bottom.

Who did it, and why?

Our intrepid birdwatcher must find a way out before the sun turns the canyon into a mortal cauldron.

A short and spirited cozy mystery introducing the energetic Lady Byrd, written by Michèle Laframboise, multi-award winner author and amateur ornithologist.

Condor Cliff

ISBN 978-1-988339-08-5 (Print)

You won't forget Malak...

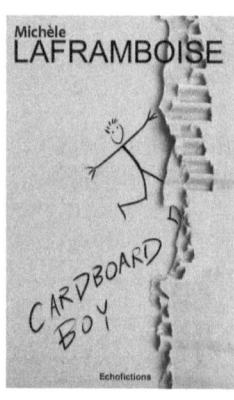

Child Labor/ Humanitarian / Sweatshops

Theo, a dispirited workplace humanitarian, audits a child worker at a cardboard factory, in a port city somewhere in Asia. He is impressed by young Malak's maturity and grit. When that boy, the same age as Theo's own son, disappears, he cannot let it rest. His quest for answers only raises more questions about the traps of structured help and acquired privilege.

An unsettling story quietly told by multiple awards-winning author Michèle Laframboise.

Cardboard Boy

ISBN 978-1-988339-22-1 (Print)

More on Echofictions.com/books

Friends' List

A story links every reader in a chain of friendship. Feel free to write your name before you give this book to someone close.

This is a unique feature of the printed edition!

Yearning for more Stories?

Michèle Laframboise's full bibliography is enough to whet any reader's appetite! Visit her author site at:
michele-laframboise.com

New stories are brewing up constantly!

To get exclusive offers, curated book reviews, advanced information on events, join Michele's happy band of readers!

michele-laframboise.com/fans

As a very busy writer, Michèle won't send mail more often than once every two months.